Who's Afraid of Swapping Spiders?

'Virginia Spider is a very special spider, a magic spider with more than a trick or two up her sleeve . . .

'You promise to look after Virginia Spider properly and you can have her. Remember though – Virginia has a particular fondness for sugar; not just an ordinary fondness like you or me having a desperate longing for sherbet fizzers or walnut whips. Without sugar she can't perform her magic. So whatever else you do, if you want to keep her happy and in the mood for a trick or two, it's very important you introduce her to the sugar bowl straight away. One last thing,' Billy added darkly, 'there's no changing your mind . . .'

Mary Welfare

Who's Afraid of Swapping Spiders?

Illustrated by
Philippe Dupasquier

MAMMOTH

First published in Great Britain 1989
by Methuen Children's Books Ltd
Published 1991 by Mammoth
an imprint of Mandarin Paperbacks
Michelin House, 81 Fulham Road, London SW3 6RB

Mandarin is an imprint of the Octopus Publishing Group,
a division of Reed International Books Limited

Text copyright © 1989 Mary Welfare
Illustrations copyright © 1989 Philippe Dupasquier

ISBN 0 7497 0113 7

A CIP catalogue record for this title
is available from the British Library

Printed in Great Britain
by Cox and Wyman Ltd, Reading, Berkshire

Contents

Chapter One

No pigs in this house

'I hate carrots,' Davey Simpkins told his mother. 'I bet they don't make you see in the dark. Owls don't eat carrots and you never hear of them bumping into trees when they're flying about at night.'

Mrs Simpkins took his plate away, giving Davey a look that said she would like to have put him in the dustbin along with the carrots. Davey knew it was not the moment to ask her, so he went to find his father.

Mr Simpkins was snoozing behind the newspaper.

'Haven't you ever heard the saying, "Children should be seen and not heard"?' he frowned.

'Yes, but why?'

Mr Simpkins put the paper down with a sigh and peered at Davey over his spectacles. 'Always asking questions, always wanting to know things. What is it this time?'

'Dad, I'd really like a pet for a companion. A penguin or a pig, though both would be nice. A penguin could live in the bath, I don't mind missing that. I could just as easily have a little wash in the kitchen sink from time to time, and give up getting myself dirty. That would please Mum. I promise the pig would be very clean. I could keep her in my bedroom.'

'You want to turn this house into a zoo?' exclaimed Mr Simpkins.

'No, no, that's exactly why they want to come here. They don't like it much in the zoo – I could tell. The penguin had a dreadfully droopy beak. And the pig was sad, too. Her tail had come all uncurled.'

'What absolute nonsense, I've never heard such an extraordinary idea. And what would your mother say? You know what she's like,' Mr Simpkins said sternly. Before Davey could think of an answer to this, his father disappeared behind the paper. Davey knew he would not get another word out of him.

'That's what comes of giving away secrets,' he said crossly to himself. 'From now on, all plans are strictly private.'

Shortly afterwards, standing at the sink, Mrs Simpkins saw a small figure creep past the kitchen door. She called out:

'Davey? What I'd like right now is a bit of help with the washing up.' No one answered. She went to the door. There was no one in sight. She shook her head.

'I've never known a boy disappear so mysteriously. He's up to something, I know he is.'

Chapter Two

The start of a secret

In the garden, out of sight of the kitchen window, Davey stopped. By his feet was a notice: 'Do Not Walk on the Grass'. A little further on was another: 'Do Not Smell the Flowers'. Davey scowled.

'I *hate* this garden; it's so horribly neat and tidy. Everything's labelled and tidied up and sprayed. Only my dad would trim the lawn with nail scissors and get down on his hands and knees to sweep the path with a

11

dustpan and brush. It's BORING!'

Next door, Billy Baggins and his tribe of brothers and sisters were playing Dangerous Games, the sort Davey was never allowed to play. Billy was standing on the branch of the old apple tree, dressed in his mother's best black Sunday coat and hat. In one hand he was waving a poker.

'Woo! woo!' he yelled at the top of his voice. 'I'm a vampire bat and I'm coming to get you.' His sisters shrieked in terror.

'Coo-ee,' shouted Davey. Billy, spotting him through a gap in the hedge, leaped down from the tree, ripping a hole in the coat and losing the hat on the way down. He didn't seem at all worried by this.

'What's up?' he asked.

When Davey invited him to squeeze through the hedge, he shook his head. 'No fear. The last time I showed my face in your garden, your dad came after me with the garden shears.' He looked closely at Davey. 'Tell me, what exactly does your dad do?'

Davey thought hard. To tell the truth he had no idea. 'I think he's probably a spy. He brings piles of paper home. Secret documents, I expect.'

Billy looked surprised. 'And your mum?' he asked. 'What d'you call her again?'

'The Fitness Fanatic. She's mad keen on jogging and health, and the right sort of food. Carrots! Yuk.'

'She sounds dangerous,' murmured Billy sympathetically.

'If only she'd stick to keep-fit,' sighed Davey, 'and forget about her pet hate.'

Billy looked interested. 'What sort of pet hate?'

'I told you – pets. She can't abide them. All shapes and sizes and smells, especially smells. She says pets have got unclean habits and nasty ways and minds of their own.' He told Billy about the penguin and the pig.

Billy wiped his nose on his sleeve. 'I wouldn't stand for it. Want me to organise a protest? We could go on a march to a Home for Unwanted Pets and rescue one, if you like.'

'It would have a miserable life. Dad would throw any pet out on its ear. And Mum would have forty fits. She screams her head off at the thought of anything with four paws and whiskers.'

'Look, I've just had a great idea,' said Billy. 'I'm, at present, the owner of something that could solve your little problem. I'd swap you for it. Trouble is, it would have to be your best belonging. How about your robot racing track?'

'You've got to be kidding, that's my most prized possession.'

'Now listen, fathead,' growled Billy, sticking his face close to Davey's, 'I'm doing

14

you a big favour. What I've got to swap is dead special. You turn it down and I'll jump on your toes.'

'Okay, okay, it's a deal. So what's this great swap of yours?'

'Not so fast, this swap's got to be a sworn secret. Tell anyone where it comes from and I'll bash your nose in.'

'Promise,' agreed Davey, 'not a squeak to a living soul.'

'Right,' said Billy, 'now here's what we do . . .'

Chapter Three

Does it bite?

Billy arranged they should meet behind the shed in Davey's garden. Davey could hardly wait. Then he started to worry about all the things that might go wrong.

'Supposing Dad suddenly decides to inspect the roses for greenfly, or the Fitness Fanatic is in the mood for a quick sprint round the lawn?'

Behind him, there was an odd scraping sound, and a crash as someone knocked

16

something to the ground. The dustbin lid! Davey held his breath in fright.

'Ouch, my knee,' a voice complained loudly and Billy Baggins scrambled over the garden wall, clutching a cardboard shoebox under one arm.

Davey opened it with trembling fingers. A black furry creature with crooked legs lay in a nest of tissue paper. Davey felt scared.

'It looks stuffed,' he whispered. He wondered whether to touch it. 'It is stuffed, isn't it? he said anxiously. Billy grinned.

'Had you fooled. Virginia is a very much alive spider. She's only in disguise as a stuffed spider.'

'Alive?' croaked Davey. 'Will she bite?'

Billy snorted with laughter. 'Virginia Spider is a very special spider, a magic spider with more than a trick or two up her sleeve. She belonged to my favourite aunt who went away on a trip to Tipperary last Hallowe'en.'

'Your aunt is a witch?' Davey grew pale. Billy grabbed hold of him by his jumper.

'Yes,' he hissed, 'but don't say I said so. My aunt taught Virginia all she knew, so not a word of her magic secrets. As far as

anyone else is concerned, Virginia is just an ordinary stuffed spider.'

Davey struggled free. 'Of course I'll keep her secrets. No one will know anything about Virginia Spider.' Then he thought. 'Gosh, won't your aunt mind if Virginia comes to live with me?'

'You promise to look after Virginia Spider properly and you can have her. Remember though – Virginia has a particular fondness for sugar; not just an ordinary fondness like you or me having a desperate longing for sherbet fizzers or walnut whips. Without sugar she can't perform her magic. So whatever else you do, if you want to keep her happy and in the mood for a trick or two, it's very important you introduce her to the sugar bowl straight away. One last thing,' Billy added darkly, 'there's no changing your mind . . .'

'Why did she leave Virginia behind, if she was so fond of her?' wondered Davey.

'Spiders don't travel well.'

'Wow,' murmured Davey. 'I wanted a pet and now I've got my own real live magic spider. I can hardly believe it.'

He was so excited he hardly paid much

attention to Billy's mysterious warning. Surely Virginia would be no trouble. All he could think was at last he had found a friend, a secret friend.

Chapter Four

A spidery trick or two

Safely in his own room, Davey lifted Virginia out of the shoebox. He wasn't frightened any more. She had a particularly agreeable sort of face, only there was a look of sadness in her tiny, shiny black eyes, as though she had lost a good friend. Was she missing the witch? Davey gently stroked the fur along her back and somehow he was sure she looked more cheerful.

He was dying to ask all about the witch

but didn't quite dare.

'Besides,' he said aloud to himself, 'I know that even magic spiders don't have conversations with seven-year-old boys.' The moment he said this, he knew it was a mistake. As she sat on the palm of his hand, Virginia Spider looked just a little cross.

'What I mean is, you're far too clever to waste your time with words,' he said hurriedly. Then he fell silent, feeling rather silly. Supposing this was just one of Billy Baggins's little jokes. Could Virginia Spider really perform magic tricks? He had never heard of such a thing before.

'I wish I could really tell,' he said aloud, slipping Virginia into his pocket before hurrying downstairs.

In the kitchen Davey put Virginia down on the table next to the teapot while he got out the biscuit tin. It was four o'clock and he was starving. The moment his back was turned he heard the pattering of tiny feet and a funny sort of scuffly scrabbling sound. Whirling round, he saw the sugar bowl had mysteriously emptied by itself. Written on the table in dusty sugary writing was a message: 'Gone for nap'. But where was Virginia?

'I don't believe it!' said Davey in amazement. 'A whole sugar bowl eaten up in one go. It's got to be Virginia. What will Billy say? I should have remembered about the sugar. And what's Mum going to say about all this mess?' He looked at the spilt sugar then ran to fetch the vacuum cleaner. Fixing on the long hose attachment with the nozzle for sucking up dust, he waved it over the table.

'Oh, no,' he gasped in horror. The nozzle had sucked up his mother's knitting. Without thinking, Davey began to pull. The harder he pulled, the faster the knitting came undone till it was lying all over the table like curly spaghetti.

'I've really done it this time,' groaned poor Davey.

Just then, something stirred under the tea cosy. Virginia had been having a quiet forty winks next to the warm teapot. Pouncing on the knitting, she seized the needles and, four pairs of legs whirring furiously, began knitting, one row plain, one row purl.

Davey's mouth fell open. On the table lay a pair of stripy pink and orange leg warmers,

beautifully knitted.

'Virginia, you're a mighty marvel.'

To celebrate, Davey and Virginia Spider had a spoonful each of Mrs Simpkins' best, very expensive coffee sugar.

'Not a word,' said Davey winking. Virginia winked back. Davey grinned. He thought his troubles were over for one day.

As he put the precious sugar back in the cupboard, Davey's eye fell on a jar of plum jam. A spoonful or two won't do any harm, he thought. But what about Virginia? Billy had said nothing about giving her plum jam. Putting her back under the tea cosy, Davey slipped on his wellies and went out into the garden.

The moment he opened the jar of jam he heard a horrid droning, whining buzz. He took a quick spoonful of jam. Then he froze. Coming straight for him was a swarm of bees, very cross bees — furious in fact. They wanted the plum jam and he had it.

'Help!' The bees were swarming all over him. 'Help!'

Somewhere above his head the leaves of the pink cherry tree stirred and out shot a black furry tornado. Davey was almost too frightened to look. A black furry beastie came swinging down on a silken thread, eight tiny spidery legs waving threateningly. Without warning, as though bewitched, the jar of plum jam flew out of Davey's hand and splatted on the ground. In a trice the bees flew after it. Virginia Spider kicked the last couple of bees out of Davey's wellies and boxed one that had got tangled up in his hair.

Davey did not stop to wonder how Virginia Spider had made the journey from the tea cosy to the top of the cherry tree. Nor did he wait to see what would happen when the bees had finished gobbling up the jam. Clutching hold of Virginia, he ran as fast as his legs would carry him into the house.

Chapter Five

A ghastly moment

'From now on I'm going to share all my secret plans with you,' said Davey, settling Virginia comfortably on his pillow. 'I'll never doubt your magic powers again.' Virginia hardly appeared to be listening. It never occurred to Davey that she might actually have secret plans of her own. He was too busy worrying about finding a safe place for her to live.

'You see, Mum's a terribly spickety-span

sort of person. One speck of dust and she's off in a frenzy with scrubbing brushes and the hoover. You'd think the Chief Inspector for Health was coming to tea, the way she goes on. I dread to think what would happen if she knew she had a spider living under her roof.'

Davey began to sort out a plan. Tucking Virginia under his jumper, he left his room. From further down the corridor, he could hear music. He smiled.

'So far, so good. That's Mum bending and stretching to Tina and the Trimettes.' He just reached the landing at the top of the stairs when the front door opened.

'Hang on tight,' he whispered to Virginia, 'I'll have to move fast. If Mum catches you in the house there'll be a frightful scene. She's definitely dangerous to spiders. In the kitchen she's got a cupboard full of nasty powders and potions, so unless you want to be sprayed with something deadly, let's not hang about. We must find you a secret hiding place.'

Tucking Virginia, for safety, up his sleeve, Davey tiptoed along the landing. By the bannisters he decided to see who was downstairs in the hall.

'That doesn't look like Dad,' he muttered.
Mr Simpkins was wearing a brown felt hat
with the brim pulled down and a dark mac
with the collar turned up, though anyone
could see it was not raining.

'What's he up to?' wondered Davey,
deeply suspicious.

Mr Simpkins happened to glance up just
then. He saw a black furry head peering out
of Davey's sleeve.

29

'What's that stuffed spider staring at? Doesn't it know it's very rude to stare?'

Virginia's black eyes seemed to glow like tiny black fires. Mr Simpkins yawned. Suddenly, he had the oddest feeling.

'What's wrong with me?' he muttered. 'I don't feel like myself at all.' He rubbed his eyes. 'Mmmm, perhaps I should have a quiet day at home. What's the point of going to work when I'm not in the mood? Proper waste of time.'

'That's very weird,' said Davey slowly. 'Dad's never missed a day's work in his life. He's hatching out a secret plot, I can tell he is. Virginia, you wicked creature, is this another of your magic tricks? I hope you know what you're doing.' Davey watched Mr Simpkins disappear into the sitting room.

'Come on,' he whispered to Virginia, 'time to tuck you away somewhere secret.'

Safe in her hiding place, Virginia Spider looked pleased with herself. Even Davey could not have guessed what was going on in her spidery mind. He thought he heard footsteps behind him. It was his mother.

Mrs Simpkins did not notice Davey as she went along to the airing cupboard to look for her favourite pink Super-stretch jogging suit. What she saw when she opened the cupboard was a trail of small brown crystals scattered over the clean folded sheets.

'What a mess. My best, most expensive coffee sugar,' she wailed. She reached further behind a pile of towels and her hand touched a hidden nest of cotton wool.

'Who's been stealing . . .' she began, putting her hand inside the nest.

She screamed, so loudly Davey nearly fell over the bannisters. His heart sank to the ends of his socks.

'Who can blame Virginia for smuggling Mum's best coffee sugar into the airing cupboard? I expect her tummy was feeling empty again and she just couldn't resist having another little taste. I don't know what all the fuss is about. Mum shouldn't mind if Virginia wants to make a comfy nest out of cotton wool. It's not as if she was planning on settling permanently in the airing cupboard. Oh dear,' he sighed, 'this is deep trouble, this is me definitely heading for the worst wigging of my life.'

Chapter Six

Look at the garden!

After the terrible shock of discovering
Virginia Spider in the airing cupboard, Mrs
Simpkins had to spend the rest of the
afternoon lying down with a wet towel
pressed to her forehead.

'Don't fret, Mum, she's perfectly safe.
Stuffed spiders don't bite. And they don't
mess up the house with dusty cobwebs and
dead flies.'

'Dead flies?' Mrs Simpkins gave a groan

and clutched her forehead. 'Just keep it well away — right out of my sight. That horrid furry thing gives me the creeps. Are you sure it's stuffed, playing tricks on me like that? If it does it again, I'll throw it down the waste-disposal unit.'

After some quick thinking Davey ran downstairs two at a time, softly, though, like a cat. In the kitchen he emptied most of a packet of cornflakes into a bowl.

'I'll leave a handful in case you're hungry,' he said gently lowering Virginia in. Her eyes twinkled gratefully from the bottom of the packet. Davey leaned over, adding in a whisper:

'I bet you're pretty good at witchy tricks and stuff like spells. I bet you're working on some magic plan right now. I bet, for a start, you could give that boring old garden out there the fright of its life; change it into something so brilliant and amazing that Billy Baggins would turn green with envy.' Listening, Virginia's eyes twinkled even more. The fun was just beginning.

As the clock struck four, Mrs Simpkins decided she felt well enough to get up. Hearing her moving about upstairs, Davey ran and quickly hid the cornflakes packet under the sink. He hoped his mother would not be seized with one of her sudden urges to wash the floor.

He need not have worried. Mrs Simpkins, going past the bedroom window, happened to glance out. And then she blinked and took a second look.

'Henry!' she uttered a strangled cry. 'Have you taken leave of your senses? What have you done to the garden?'

Wondering what all the fuss was about, Davey went to have a look for himself.

'It's brilliant, Virginia,' he gasped. 'It's the most wonderful garden I've ever seen.'

The roses had grown and grown and grown, into a wild wood, almost hiding the potting shed. The greenhouse had mysteriously disappeared. Where it should have been, stood the smallest glass castle, all lit up with fairy lights and clockwork singing birds. Right in the middle of the lawn, once Mr Simpkins' pride and joy, was an amazing spaceship sunhouse, slowly revolving like a merry-go-round. Nearby, more amazing still, was a scarlet and gold Chinese pagoda.

'Wow!' exclaimed Davey excitedly. 'It's a real helter-skelter. And look at that!' Down the helter-skelter, flying faster than the clockwork birds, came Mr Simpkins himself.

'Dad should be hating all of it. And there he is, grinning from ear to ear. It's not just the garden you've put a spell on, Virginia Spider. I've never seen him like this before.'

Mrs Simpkins, however, had seen more than enough. She sat down heavily on the kitchen chair.

'Make me a cup of tea, please, with lots of sugar in it.'

'What about your diet, Mum?' asked Davey.

'What diet?' Mrs Simpkins was too dazed to think straight.

'Quite right,' said Davey. 'It wasn't doing you any good.' He stirred in six spoonfuls of sugar. His mother still didn't look quite her old self. 'Don't worry about the garden,' he said, trying to cheer her up, 'you'll like this new one much better when you get used to it.' Mrs Simpkins shook her head.

She took a sip of tea and almost choked. 'This tea is awful, really terrible.' Davey took the cup from her and was about to pour the tea down the sink when his eye fell on something black and furry crawling up the pot of ivy on the windowsill. He gulped in horror.

'Virginia, for goodness sake, how did you get there? Mum will go berserk if she catches you, she'll hit the roof.'

'Davey?' he heard his mother say. 'What are you doing speaking to that pot of ivy? It's bad enough already, what with the shock of finding that frightful stuffed spidery beast in the airing cupboard, and your father turning the garden into an amusement park.'

Mrs Simpkins sighed. 'Not so long ago, we were a perfectly ordinary, respectable family. Nothing peculiar, nothing really interesting ever happened to us. Now, I never know what's going to happen next, it's all gone topsy-turvy. It's like living in a Haunted House of Horrors.' She stopped, struck again by a sudden thought.

'What will the neighbours think? You know what a gossip that old busybody . . .'

Just then the front door bell rang.

Chapter Seven

Bugs and beasties

On the doorstep stood a large lady in a tweed suit.

'Ooops!' said Davey pulling a face, 'Mrs Parkinson-Porter. This means trouble.' There had been a bit of a scene after Mrs Parkinson-Porter's dog, who was dreadfully short-sighted, had mistaken Davey's mother, out jogging in her fluffy lambswool track-suit, for a sheep. Ever since then the two neighbours had not been on speaking terms.

'On behalf of the Town and County Ladies' Committee, I've come to lodge a complaint,' announced Mrs Parkinson-Porter, in her most bossy voice. Mrs Simpkins smiled a smile sweeter than syrup.

'I was about to have a cup of tea.' She got out the best china. 'Would you care for an iced-cake fancy, or would you prefer a raspberry Slimmybic?' she said, passing the plate.

'Mrs Simpkins,' replied Mrs Parkinson-Porter stiffly, refusing both. 'About this monstrous development – those ghastly constructions that have sprung up in your garden – the Committee and I feel most strongly . . .'

She seemed to have forgotten what she was going to say. Underneath the cup Mrs Simpkins had just picked up was a huge slimy black slug. It made straight for Mrs Parkinson-Porter's lap. Davey's mother gave a stifled shriek, Mrs Parkinson-Porter gasped. Davey's eyes were like saucers. He only hoped the two ladies would not notice a fat green caterpillar inching its way up the tablecloth.

Mrs Parkinson-Porter was staring at

something quite different. A whole lot of funny grubby footprints had suddenly appeared in the butter. Across the table were tiny trails of sugar. Mrs Parkinson-Porter's face froze in disgust, noticing that the chair she was sitting on was covered in fine sticky threads. Cobwebs!

'And what's *this*? She looked more closely. 'A baby furry octopus? My socks!' she yelped, leaping out of her chair. 'It's a giant killer tarantula. It's about to attack me.'

'It's only Virginia, my pet stuffed spider,' Davey assured her, 'making one of her guest appearances.'

'Well, this guest has had enough,' snapped Mrs Parkinson-Porter. 'She looks far too cunning for a stuffed spider. There's more to this than meets the eye, if you ask me.' She picked up her hat. There, nestled up amongst the fake felt flowers, was the biggest cockroach she had ever seen.

Mrs Simpkins closed her eyes in despair. She heard the front door bang shut.

'Has she gone?' she asked faintly. Very slowly she opened her eyes. 'Davey?' she said, her voice ominously sharp, 'did you bring those creepy crawlies into the house?'

'No,' said Davey truthfully, 'but I know someone who did.' Naughty spider, he groaned to himself, this appetite for sugar is getting us into a whole heap of trouble. Conjuring up those beasties was a wonderful magic prank, but what am I going to do with them all? It's definitely not safe here.

Mrs Simpkins shivered. 'This house is haunted. Everywhere I go that dratted stuffed thing plays tricks on me. I'm sure it's bewitched. I always said never trust a spider. I can't abide anything with four legs, and that Virginia creature's got eight, not to mention filthy cobwebby habits and a sweet tooth. It's all her fault, isn't it? After what happened at tea-time, that awful old bossy-boots, Mrs Parkinson-Porter, is bound to stir up trouble. Davey?' she said crossly. 'Are you listening?'

But Davey had gone. He had just had a terrific idea.

Chapter Eight

A fright in the potting shed

'Wotcherupto?' called out Billy Baggins, spying Davey in the garden. They met halfway through the hedge. Billy was amazed.

'Your garden! Wow, what a tip. It's smashing, a great improvement. But what's your dad up to, exactly? Is that a lighthouse over there? It's kind of crooked.'

'It was the greenhouse. It's a castle now.'

'Mmmm,' said Billy thoughtfully. 'How's

46

Virginia?'

'Fine,' replied Davey airily. He wondered if he should tell Billy his plan. This is a desperate situation, he thought to himself. Every time I turn my back Virginia Spider is up to mischief of one kind or another. Here I am, landed with a household of uninvited creepy crawlies. I'm going to need help. Billy's my best friend and what are best friends for when you're in a terrible spot of bother?

'Billy,' he said slowly, 'fancy being a Deputy Zoo Keeper? I'm going to have an animal sanctuary here in the garden. You could help me.'

'What? With your dad on the rampage every time I so much as poke my head through the hedge? Have you thought about the Fitness Fanatic and her pet phobia, having forty fits whenever anything with four paws and whiskers goes near her?'

'It's dead secret. You spill the beans and Virginia will jump over the hedge and bewitch you, like she's bewitched Dad.'

'Ah, so Virginia's up to her old tricks again, is she? I should have known she wouldn't be able to behave herself for very long.'

'She's terrific. I haven't had such fun for ages.' Davey explained about Mrs Parkinson-Porter and the mysterious invasion of bugs and beasties, and all the fuss and commotion it had caused.

'I've moved them to the rockery, the only safe place left.'

'And Virginia? Where've you put her?'

'She's dozing in one of Dad's welly boots.'

'Is that wise? She could get horribly squashed. You put her somewhere else and I'll go hunting for some specimens for the zoo.'

In no time he was back.

'I've written some labels for each sort of animal. Here's one: "The most miniature dinosaur in captivity — very rare".'

'But what is it?' said Davey excitedly.

'A lizard, actually. I found him in the coal-scuttle, though I daresay he'll be very happy moving to the rock garden.'

'And what's that?'

'"Great Warty Toad — flesh eating (specially dead flies)".'

'Yuk,' declared Davey. 'How about

frogs? We could dig a pond and fill it with frog families.'

They had entirely forgotten about Mr Simpkins, who had, that very moment, gone into the potting shed, seized by yet another plan for a fantastic construction.

'I'll knock this down and build an underground laboratory. I'll start at once.'

Then he heard, softly at first, a snuffly,

sniffly sound, getting louder. A deep grunting snoring. Mr Simpkins felt trembly at the knees. An invisible snoring! He took a step forward and bent down. Tucked up, side by side, on the shelf next to the potting compost were two fast-asleep hedgehogs.

'Bloomin' begonias! How did those prickly pests get there?' Mr Simpkins looked round for his pipe. These days Mrs Simpkins was forever nagging him to give up such a nasty filthy habit. Whenever he wanted a secret smoke he had to slip down to the potting shed. Hoping a quiet puff would soon solve the problem of where to get rid of the hedgehogs, somewhere far, far away, Mr Simpkins reached for the tobacco pouch lying near by. He frowned.

'Who's been chewing my tobacco?' Just as he was about to pick the pouch up, it moved. 'Come out, whoever you are,' he commanded, 'with your hands up.'

After a slight pause, Virginia Spider emerged, shame-faced, looking rather sick from eating the tobacco, with all eight legs in the air. Mr Simpkins was so shocked he swore then and there never to smoke again.

'A stuffed spider with a taste for tobacco

and a mind of its own,' he muttered. All at once he looked at all the weird and wonderful buildings in the garden, as though waking from a dream.

'Did I do all that?' he groaned. 'Great Garden Disasters, what could I have been thinking of?' He rushed outside.

'Davey, come here at once. I'm warning you, remove this spider before she gets chopped up in the cement mixer. And what's that you're hiding behind your back? Show me.'

Slowly, Davey held out his hand. Mr Simpkins gasped.

'A rodent! A verminous little beast.'

'It's only a mouse. It's totally harmless. In fact, it's dead. Billy brought it over in a trap. We were going to give it a decent burial in the rock garden with a wreath.'

'This isn't funny, Davey. I'm not laughing. Tomorrow, first thing, we're going to have a few changes around here. Starting with Virginia Spider. There's something about her I don't like.'

Chapter Nine

Watch out, Virginia!

'Something's wrong,' thought Davey all of a sudden. He had been pulling on his socks when he had this terrible feeling that Virginia Spider was in trouble. He ran to the window. Out in the garden disaster had struck.

A little earlier, Mr Simpkins, still not in the best of moods from the day before, had been shaving. Glancing out at the garden, he noticed on the patch of grass which was all that was left of the lawn, a movement as though the ground was being disturbed by a minor earthquake. The grass heaved and shook as something wriggled along under the earth.

'Perishing moles,' he yelled, 'just you wait.' With a growl of rage and a beard of shaving cream still sticking to his chin, Mr Simpkins rushed downstairs, seized the frying pan and flew into the garden. In a fury he began walloping the ground.

A few feet away, out of a newly dug-up molehill, shot five or six frantically waving legs.

'That's no mole,' gasped Davey, still looking out of the window. In a flash he was outside too, just in time to see Virginia Spider scuttling away, heading for the safety of Billy Baggins' garden.

'Virginia, don't go,' he called after her. 'Please stay.' But it made no difference. She was gone.

'Virginia was my best friend, and you've scared her away,' he cried angrily. Mr Simpkins wagged a finger.

'She's no friend of mine. Besides, I'm not having this garden turned into a safari park.

Everywhere I look I find nasty creepy crawlies. I'm going to launch an all-out attack on vermin; I'm going to call in the Pest Control Officer. That spidery beast will be the first to go. She's responsible for all this madness.' He waved a hand at the crooked castle, the revolving spaceship sunhouse, the Chinese pagoda helter-skelter, and groaned, 'I must have been off my head. It's all coming down.

'As for your pet sanctuary, I shall put down poison and pellets and powders. I'll put up barbed wire and an electric fence against intruders. There'll be bird scarers and cat frighteners and traps . . . even the worms in the ground won't be safe.'

Goodness knows what other awful ideas he might have come up with next if Mrs Simpkins hadn't called from the house.

'You've got a visitor, Henry.' Mr Simpkins turned and his face fell. By the kitchen door a man, in a smart pin-striped suit, stood waiting.

'The Boss! Wondering where I've got to these last few days. There'll be talk of early retirement. I'm done for, finished.'

Following him inside, Davey thought he had never seen his father so down-in-the-dumps. What could be wrong?

'Mum,' he whispered, 'is Dad about to be taken away for being a spy?'

'A spy? What nonsense are you talking about? Your father's a second-hand car salesman.'

'I'm afraid my mind hasn't been on my work lately,' said Mr Simpkins, shaking his head sadly. 'I think I've been bewitched by a stuffed spider by the name of Virginia.'

'Hmmm, an odd story, to be sure,'

murmured the Boss, 'perhaps a long holiday, a very long holiday . . .'

Mrs Simpkins sighed. 'The garden used to be so nice, so wonderfully neat and tidy. Not a blade of grass or a petal out of place. It was Henry's pride and joy. I simply don't know what's come over him. Just lately he's taken to getting up in the middle of the night to saw up stuff in the garage. Or what used to be the garage. Looks more like a House of Horrors after what he's done to it. You should just see the dreadful . . .'

Filled with curiosity, the Boss decided to have a look for himself. He was thrilled.

'Why didn't you ever tell me, Henry? What talent! A brilliant scheme, so original, so inspired. Gardens can be boring, and if I remember, yours was one of the most boring.

'You come and see me tomorrow and we'll sort out a new future for you. It's going to be a splendid success: Henry Simpkins, Designer of Incredibly Amazing Gardens. Now don't forget, my office at nine o'clock sharp.'

Chapter Ten

An unexpected visitor

Davey took a deep breath.

'Couldn't you ever learn to get fond of a stuffed spider? Couldn't you try? Perhaps you could try speaking nicely to her.' Mrs Simpkins stopped in the middle of fifty press-ups.

'I've never been on speaking terms with a spider,' she said doubtfully, 'and Virginia's been very naughty.'

'She didn't mean any real harm,' a voice

said from the doorway. Everyone jumped.

The most beautiful person Davey had ever seen stood in the doorway, a tall lady with long hair like black silk, dressed in a deep-blue frock spangled with silver stars and golden moons. He was lost for words.

'I was just making a cup of tea,' Mrs Simpkins croaked.

'Do sit here,' said Mr Simpkins jumping to his feet.

Ignoring them both, the stranger went across to Davey.

'I've come to say hello, and Virginia's come to say goodbye, and sorry.' She smiled and showed Davey her pocket where, curled up, comfortable and happy, was Virginia. 'She's coming with me to Basingstoke, to run a home for elderly cats. You must visit us, now you're a special friend.'

Davey couldn't believe it. 'You're Billy's aunt. The witch!'

Miss Twilight put a finger to her lips.

'That's me,' she whispered. 'But maybe we should keep quiet about that.' She turned to Mr and Mrs Simpkins.

'Let me introduce myself; Miss Twilight, doctor of medicine and, ah, specialist in rare and secret skills. Please forgive Virginia Spider. All those little secrets I taught her seem to have gone to her head.'

'Well, well, well,' laughed Mr Simpkins, 'some pretty odd things have been going on here, but this certainly is a surprise. A very nice surprise.'

'I shall miss Virginia,' said Davey. 'I was getting very fond of her.'

Mrs Simpkins coughed. She suddenly looked ashamed.

'Excuse me, er, Miss Twilight, I don't mean to be impertinent but as you have a degree in medicine, could you cure me of my pet phobia?'

Miss Twilight's eyes twinkled.

'Of course.' She searched about in her other pocket. 'Here, try this, it's absolute magic: pussy willow and clover syrup. Works wonders. Ten drops in your tea should do the trick.'

She was interrupted by a faint whimper.

'Oh, yes, I forgot about him. He seems to have followed me in. Is he yours? A bit runtish, poor thing. Needs feeding up, I'd say.'

They all looked. Round the door, a

pathetic face showed itself. A short-eared, long-tailed mongrel crept into the room and lay at Mrs Simpkins' feet. She began to tremble. At that same moment, Virginia Spider crawled out of Miss Twilight's pocket, and fixed Mrs Simpkins with a beady eye. Mrs Simpkins swallowed hard. She saw Davey's face light up. At last she spoke.

'We could swap him for Virginia Spider, I suppose.'

Miss Twilight nodded her head graciously. 'An excellent idea,' she said.

A Selected List of Fiction from Mammoth

While every effort is made to keep prices low, it is sometimes necessary to increase prices at short notice. Mammoth Books reserves the right to show new retail prices on covers which may differ from those previously advertised in the text or elsewhere.

The prices shown below were correct at the time of going to press.

☐	7497 0366 0	**Dilly the Dinosaur**	Tony Bradman	£1.99
☐	7497 0021 1	**Dilly and the Tiger**	Tony Bradman	£1.99
☐	7497 0137 4	**Flat Stanley**	Jeff Brown	£1.99
☐	7497 0048 3	**Friends and Brothers**	Dick King-Smith	£1.99
☐	7497 0054 8	**My Naughty Little Sister**	Dorothy Edwards	£1.99
☐	416 86550 X	**Cat Who Wanted to go Home**	Jill Tomlinson	£1.99
☐	7497 0166 8	**The Witch's Big Toe**	Ralph Wright	£1.99
☐	7497 0218 4	**Lucy Jane at the Ballet**	Susan Hampshire	£2.25
☐	416 03212 5	**I Don't Want To!**	Bel Mooney	£1.99
☐	7497 0030 0	**I Can't Find It!**	Bel Mooney	£1.99
☐	7497 0032 7	**The Bear Who Stood on His Head**	W. J. Corbett	£1.99
☐	416 10362 6	**Owl and Billy**	Martin Waddell	£1.75
☐	416 13822 5	**It's Abigail Again**	Moira Miller	£1.75
☐	7497 0031 9	**King Tubbitum and the Little Cook**	Margaret Ryan	£1.99
☐	7497 0041 6	**The Quiet Pirate**	Andrew Matthews	£1.99
☐	7497 0064 5	**Grump and the Hairy Mammoth**	Derek Sampson	£1.99

All these books are available at your bookshop or newsagent, or can be ordered direct from the publisher. Just tick the titles you want and fill in the form below.

Mandarin Paperbacks, Cash Sales Department, PO Box 11, Falmouth, Cornwall TR10 9EN.

Please send cheque or postal order, no currency, for purchase price quoted and allow the following for postage and packing:

UK   80p for the first book, 20p for each additional book ordered to a maximum charge of £2.00.

BFPO   80p for the first book, 20p for each additional book.

Overseas   £1.50 for the first book, £1.00 for the second and 30p for each additional book including Eire   thereafter.

NAME (Block letters) ....

ADDRESS ....

....

....